Three Tales

Three Tales

MINASU

CLOISTER HOUSE PRESS

First published in the United Kingdom in 2022 by
The Cloister House Press

ISBN 978-1-913460-51-8

Contents

Soul Sweeper

A worn soul swept the restaurant floor at the end of the day. This activity consumed every last sinew of Mi Na's body. He dashed about the space, back and forth, until it was spotless and then he mopped with greater will still. When it was time to lock up, the urge to leave was so strong that simply turning the key and stepping outside the front door did nothing to relieve him. He stood waiting to be washed by a wave of euphoria but it did not come. Alarmed, he unlocked the door and went back inside the restaurant to clean it all over again. But no matter how much he cleaned he was not pricked even by the edge of enthusiasm. 'I must leave now,' he thought. 'The restaurant, this town and everybody in it. I must go to a place far away, where sweeping and mopping are a distant memory.' Opportunity, faith and love had fallen by the wayside and it was the end of this journey to recapture them to a degree more pure than ever before. He slept soundly that night, dreaming of a tropical island thick with jungle, its inhabitants going about their daily lives where the lush trees parted and made way to expanses of sandy beaches.

The morning sun rose and he informed his deputy of the plan, who greeted the idea with confusion and contempt. Failing to dissuade Mi Na, he finally conceded that this was a necessary venture.

'When will you return?' he asked.

Soon, not-for-a-while and never became one in Mi Na's mind. 'I don't know,' he said. By midday he had informed each and every one of those close to him of his decision. His mother was anxious and warned of the dangers ahead, his brother dismayed and his lover heartbroken. Numb to all of this, Mi Na sought a semblance of calm in the few possessions he packed in a small leather bag. Among an assortment of clothes, each item rolled up into a ball no larger than a fist, nestled a small book containing the writings of a monk. 'I will understand these words,' he said to himself. 'To observe nature and describe it so plainly as to capture all of life's wonders at once. How such insight dangles over my poor head as a low-hanging fruit bobbing stubbornly beyond my grasp!'

A train pulled into the station and Mi Na travelled south through the countryside. The sun's rays sparkled among the flooded paddy fields and the young man felt sure that this was the most beautiful moment to which he had ever been privy. He retrieved a pen and notebook from his bag and pondered the disconnect between his life at home and the harmony of the elements with the farmland. 'A sodden field owes its fate to the rains, to no man does it yield, this sodden field.' Pained by the trite nature of his words he punished himself by thinking of nothing but nothingness for the rest of the ride. Even this was no mean feat. Mi Na grappled with rushing thoughts about man's neglect of nature, flooding and the miraculous properties of skin until his head finally fell into his lap.

The train driver woke Mi Na at the end of the line. The terminus stood on a hill that overlooked a turquoise sea and a small harbour of exactly one boat. 'Hurry and you will make the next trip out to the island!' called the driver. Mi Na held his bag to his chest and ran down the hill as quickly as his legs could carry him. At the base of the hill lay a creaking wooden boardwalk where fishermen smoked. 'Please come along now,' said a boatman. Mi Na thanked him and climbed aboard. Sacks of rice sat in the bay of the boat and a disparate band of travellers gathered around them. Some turned to the sea and others to their comrades but Mi Na was transfixed by the sacks of rice. 'The poetry lies in the process,' he thought. 'What are the paddy fields and the farmers without the sacks and the boats and the boatmen?' A seagull circled the boat and came to rest on the bow. She stood with such poise that no one aboard could fail to notice. Even the boatmen saluted the bird as she flew between the rice sacks and inspected them one by one to rapturous applause. When she was done, she flew to the stern and stayed there for the duration of the ride.

Longtail boats anchored at the shore cast their evening shadows and fluffy clouds danced with the evening sun over the sea. The boat was tied up and everyone disembarked. No sooner had Mi Na felt the sand between his toes than a young boy cried out to him – 'Hey you!' Startled, Mi Na realised that he had forgotten how to speak on the voyage. 'Do you want fried noodles or noodle soup?' Mi Na repeated the words noodle and soup after the boy. 'Do you want chicken or pork or beef?' Pork, please. 'Do you want water or cola or iced coffee?' Water, please. 'Please take a seat.' It was only then that Mi Na noticed three benches lined up on the beach. A single space remained on the middle one. With the words noodle and soup and pork and water rattling around in his ears Mi

Na observed the boy. 'Never have I seen such a command of a restaurant,' he thought. Remembering his own restaurant he shook his head in shame. 'It is true that this boy only offers two dishes, which are practically the same, and that three benches is a small capacity, but never mind it! He is working alone and cannot be more than eight years old.' Chicken or pork or beef and water or cola or iced coffee became all that Mi Na knew. The boy ran up to the cauldron of steaming noodles stirred dutifully by his mother and back to the benches relaying bowl after bowl of fried noodles and noodle soup with chicken or pork or beef. Carrying the drinks was so effortless for the boy that he skipped between tables and climbed among customers to give them water or cola or iced coffee. The food was delicious. Mi Na chewed up the noodles and slurped down the soup almost as soon as the glorious scent had wafted under his nostrils. 'Three dollar fifty, please.' The boy stood still and smiled sweetly. 'The humility of this child is unlike anything I have ever seen,' thought Mi Na. 'I must reward him at once!' And so he handed over a five dollar bill and explained that the change was for him and his mother. The boy shrieked with delight and made for his mother's arms, who cradled her son with boundless joy.

That evening the island cooled and Mi Na found a hut to rest in by sundown. All manner of creatures knocked about in the rickety old hut from bugs and rats to lizards and bats and this continued through the night. Despite the cacophony of jungle noise surrounding Mi Na he could not hear any of it. All he could think of was the boy. 'To call him a boy would be to pay him a disservice. He is an adult in any meaningful sense of the word. He runs his restaurant with consummate skill. How can one achieve this level of professionalism at such an age? Love. Love is the only conceivable answer.' With

4

that thought, Mi Na decided that he would eat fried noodles in the morning and noodle soup in the evening as long as he remained on the island. Each time the boy would command his space with greater authority. One time he apologised for the chickens had not yet been killed that day. Another time he berated a fully grown man for killing a chicken in the wrong way. 'Not like that! Like this!' he would shout. The man appeared to be the boy's father and one morning Mi Na decided to introduce himself.

'Hello, sir,' he said to the man.

'Hello,' the man replied.

'Your boy is one of a kind.'

At this the man recoiled and revealed a toothy grin. 'Thank you for your help,' he said.

Mi Na explained that he was the one who should be grateful, for the man's boy had inspired him and made his journey worthwhile.

'Thank you for your help,' the man repeated.

'What is his name?' Mi Na asked.

'Su Rong.'

Mi Na ate his noodles and Su Rong appeared before him when the bowl was empty. 'Three dollar fifty, please,' he stated, like clockwork. Checking his pockets, it occurred to Mi Na that on this occasion he only had three dollars and fifty cents to offer the boy. He acknowledged that his tipping had become customary and so he broke it to him as gently as he could – 'No tip this morning, double tip this evening.' At that Su Rong let out a primordial scream and sobbed to his heart's content. His veneer of composure par excellence had been shattered into a thousand irreconcilable pieces. 'I must leave now,' thought Mi Na. Numbed once more he packed his bag, locked his hut and boarded the next boat back to the mainland. He did not marvel at the sacks of rice, nor did he wonder at a seagull. Instead he mulled over the illusion of purity that had been wrested from him. 'The island was a mistake but I cannot return to sweeping. My soul cannot sweep any longer. I must continue this venture.' The train was waiting at the station when the boat pulled into the harbour on the mainland. Mi Na held his bag to his chest and ran up the hill as fast as his legs could carry him. He boarded the train and travelled north through the countryside. 'To the mountains,' he said to himself. 'That is where truth can be found.'

The train pulled up at the northernmost stop. At this juncture in the valley the milky brown river flowed slowly. 'This evening will be devoid of cool air,' said Mi Na to himself. 'Perhaps there will be some freshness in the deep of the night.' This time he did not concern himself with finding a hut before dark. Walking along the riverbank, he circled the village again and again. 'He walked alone through the night, seeking fresh air with all of his might.' Mi Na was bothered by the ordinariness of his poetry but he would not punish himself for it. 'The river moves slowly but it will make it to the sea,' he pondered. Once he had been able to inhale a breath of fresh air he found a hut to stay in by midnight. Off the beaten track this hut was part of a small cluster. A swing swayed in a courtyard decorated with potted plants and covered by palm trees. Mi Na rested on the swing and just when he was on the verge of drifting away he was greeted by a young man about his own age. 'Hello, I am Xeng Xong, the caretaker. Could I take your bag and bring you coffee?' In no mood to sleep, Mi Na accepted the offer of coffee but insisted he carry his own bag. Xeng Xong smiled sweetly and showed his guest to his hut. Sitting on the edge of the bed, Mi Na rambled to himself,

'Beware of those with sweet smiles singing songs about coffee, he'd better not be wretched too lest I feel the urge to flee...'

Xeng Xong knocked on the door. 'Please come in,' Mi Na called. The caretaker gestured to his guest to join him in the courtyard. The coffee was ready. The pair of them sat on the swing and let it sway slowly back and forth. After several minutes of silence Xeng Xong was moved to speak.

'Please teach me,' he said in a hushed tone.

'There is nothing I can teach you,' replied Mi Na wearily.

'Teach me to speak like you.'

As far as Mi Na could tell, Xeng Xong was able to articulate everything he needed to. 'You already speak like I do.'

Xeng Xong hunched over and stared at his hands. 'I can speak to guests when they arrive and leave. I can take your bag and bring you coffee. But that is all.' Looking over at him Mi Na noticed that Xeng Xong had exceptionally large hands for a man of his size. He was short and lean. 'My hands are the hands of my father,' he said.

'Are you from the mountains?' This was the first statement to evade Xeng Xong's comprehension. It was then that Mi Na became captivated once more. 'I must be understood by this young man – this good man! All he has done is what I have asked, yet here I sit assuming the futility of it all. But why? This malaise has been brought on by a worthless setback. No – fatigue is the culprit! Well, the coffee is kicking in, so let's do this!'

Xeng Xong and Mi Na stayed up all night talking to each other about the worlds they had left behind to meet that night in the courtyard. Setting off long before sunrise, Xeng Xong would say good bye to his parents and trek down towards the valley. On his way he would practise mental arithmetic and ponder the questions of science. School ran from sunrise till mid-afternoon. Then he would swim in the river with his classmates and take a meal before crossing the village for the night shift at the inn.

'But the river is muddy,' noted Mi Na.

'Some parts are clear.'

Mi Na wondered how the river was affected by the seasons but Xeng Xong did not understand what he meant by this. 'Well, I am from a town on the other side of the mountains. There, we have four phases of weather each year.'

This seemed impossible to Xeng Xong, who proclaimed, 'There is a rainy season and there is a sunny season.' It was true. Rain and sun are pretty much ubiquitous on this planet of ours.

'But,' continued Mi Na, 'where I'm from we have a snowy season and a season when the leaves of the trees turn from green to brown.'

This astonished Xeng Xong. He had heard of snow and the process of water turning to ice at freezing temperatures was familiar to him from his studies. But green leaves turning brown? This was beyond his understanding. Mi Na explained that the tree itself does not die when this happens.

'Only the leaves die?' asked Xeng Xong.

Mi Na smiled. 'Yes, just like hair that falls out of your head.'

As the days passed the young men bonded over their diverse backgrounds. Mi Na dazzled Xeng Xong with tales of cities comprising millions of citizens. The sheer number of zeroes, all six of them and sometimes seven, made Xeng Xong smile a great deal. When he found out that there was a country, nay two countries, each playing host to over a billion people, he was blown away by a crescendo of hearty laughter.

'But what of your home?' Mi Na asked. 'How is it there?'

Xeng Xong slumped back on the swing. 'When my mother

falls ill, my father sacrifices a chicken. When my father falls ill, my mother sacrifices another chicken. Many chickens die like this where I am from.'

Mi Na wondered what his friend thought of this purported correlation.

'We get better after the chicken is sacrificed but I think we would get better anyway,' Xeng Xong pondered.

'It is a tradition,' thought Mi Na. 'We have traditions too,' he said. 'Where I'm from,' he began, 'we ask ourselves why.'

Xeng Xong did not understand. 'Why?' he repeated.

'Yes, why. Why are we here? What is the purpose for all of this?'

Xeng Xong's confusion showed no sign of abating.

'Put it this way,' Mi Na continued. 'The sun causes heat. It is the reason plants and trees grow. You could say that the sun is why we are here.' Xeng Xong nodded attentively. 'Now, given this, I put to you Xeng Xong of the mountains, why are we here?'

After a moment's pause he replied, 'I am here because of my mother and father.' He was correct. His mother and father were indeed his reason to be.

'But what of them?' Mi Na pressed on.

'My mother is here because of her mother and father and my father is here because of his mother and father,' Xeng Xong reasoned.

'Yes! But what of their mothers and fathers?' The men gave each other a knowing look and laughed wildly all at once. Then a serious expression painted itself over Xeng Xong's face.

'We come from monkeys,' he concluded.

Mi Na felt like he had been punched squarely between the eyes but adrenaline coursed through him and he felt nothing. 'Did you learn that at school?' he asked.

'No,' replied Xeng Xong.

That night Mi Na lay on his back in bed. The sounds of wildlife around him passed through him as one. 'Xeng Xong is a phenomenon,' he thought. 'He deduced the theory of evolution as though it were a matter of pure logic, though I'm sure his exposure to a multitude of animals has something to do with it. Regardless! I am sated at last. I shall reside at this inn till the end of my days and teach Xeng Xong everything I know. He does not even demand a cent for my wisdom. Oh, how much more pure could an exchange be than one in which money does not change hands!'

Mi Na awoke to the sound of clucking hens. He spent his day as he had become accustomed to, walking alongside the milky brown river, circling the village again and again until the deep of the night, for which he waited with bated breath. When it was cool enough to inhale the succulent night air without inhibition, he returned to the courtyard to meet with Xeng Xong. Tonight, however, the caretaker had changed his tune.

'What business do you do in your town?' he asked.

Mi Na told him that he had a restaurant and that he was enjoying some time away from the place. It was in good hands.

'You make money in the big town from the restaurant business. Here, there is no money. I learn math and science at school. I learn to speak better with you. All of my friends do something like this. But in the end we are poor and the government is rich. Why?' Xeng Xong launched that why deep into Mi Na's heart with all of the skill of someone who had wielded that weapon his whole life.

'That is a very big why!'

'Why?' the caretaker repeated. Mi Na went to great lengths to explain supply and demand and capitalism and socialism and corruption and justice and good and evil but none of this satisfied Xeng Xong. 'Why?' he repeated.

'I'm sorry, I have no answer for you,' Mi Na replied. From that moment onwards the men would no longer speak as equals. Xeng Xong insisted that he would leave his home and join Mi Na on his travels. They would visit the world's great cities and make a fortune. Mi Na shook his head in shame. 'I must leave now,' he thought.

And just like that he packed his bag and left the following morning. One recollection of his travails mopping the floor at his restaurant spurred him on. 'I am not yet ready to hop on top of a mop. Ah, blasted poetry – how you flatter to deceive! The solution does not lie with words at all! Nor with anything comprised of them – theory and reason be damned!' It became his sole mission to find a tuk-tuk driver who would take him westwards to the monastery deep in the rainforest. In any case, there was no use in waiting for one, so Mi Na set off on foot to the west. Soon he was surrounded only by mountains and valleys and no people at all. When he passed someone who sold water or rice the dollars he offered them were met with bemusement. Mi Na possessed one hundred and fifty thousand of the local currency but decided not to spend it on water or rice. 'If I see a driver I will need every last bit of it,' he thought. A tuk-tuk driver rode past Mi Na and called out to him. He insisted on three hundred thousand of the local currency but this was too much for Mi Na. It was not because he deemed the value of his labour to be less than three hundred thousand but because he only had one hundred and fifty thousand. This fact was lost on many a driver until one old man in a vehicle that had seen better days pulled up by Mi Na. There were no longer roads at this stage of the route.

'One hundred thousand for you,' said Mi Na.

'OK,' replied the driver. 'Where?'

After some confusion about the purpose of a journey to a monastery, Mi Na had had enough. 'There is no reason for my journey. I simply must go to the monastery, at once!'

The tuk-tuk hurtled between potholes as the old man pushed his vehicle to its limit. Surrounded by motorcycles and scooters, the limitations of this beaten up tuk-tuk were all too clear. They rolled down a dusty track shrouded in its entirety by tree cover. Little light penetrated the force field of the forest though this did not deter the elderly driver who seemed to revel in the challenge. Eventually they rolled up limply to the foot of the monastery. Mi Na was covered from head to toe in orange dust. 'At least we made it by sundown,' he said to himself. He gave the driver a hundred thousand and he made off with it into the night. 'It is not Xeng Xong's fault,' thought Mi Na. 'After all, why must I burden those so young and innocent with the task of fulfilling my nightmarishly whimsical fetishes of the mind! Why ever would I do such a thing! Why, indeed.' His stream of consciousness was halted by chanting. A smooth melody slipped out of the temple and imbued Mi Na with a sense of peace unlike any he had experienced before. A monk in an orange robe descended the steps of the temple and stood in front of Mi Na.

'You come to stay with us?' he asked.

'Yes, I came to stay with you.'

The monk studied the outsider through the darkness. 'You come to meditate with us?' he asked.

'Yes, I came to meditate with you.'

It was agreed that the best thing for Mi Na to do was wash himself and rest before the gong would sound several hours before sunrise the next day.

'What happens when I hear the gong?' asked Mi Na.

'You come to temple for morning prayer and meditation.'

By the time the gong sounded Mi Na had been lying awake for a while. He had spent the night cleaning himself as swiftly and thoroughly as the facilities permitted. A small bowl floated atop a larger bowl itself filled to the brim with water. This water would be replaced manually by the unsteady trickle of a rusty tap. The hole in the bathroom floor would function as a toilet. 'It is helpful that it flushes with two small bowlfuls of water,' thought Mi Na. He napped intermittently but had woken up each time with aches and pains. 'It is because I am not accustomed to sleeping on the floor,' he mused. 'I move in my sleep when I sleep in a bed because I will spring back into place from whichever position I please. Only when I can sleep on my back with total stillness will I awake pain-free.' All of these thoughts mingled in the mind of Mi Na against a cacophony of jungle noise louder than the noise of the island and louder still than the noise of the valley. He made his way from the hut to the temple by memory as only darkness pervaded the forest.

Upon reaching the temple Mi Na stopped in his tracks at the sound of a single monk chanting. 'I should enter slowly,' he thought. Climbing the stairs one by one a vast hall revealed itself to him, its walls adorned with all manner of decoration and splendour. A large monk, who seemed to be an important figure in the monastery, sat at the front of the hall cross-legged, orange clad, his back to an array of dazzling paintings and statuettes. He looked across the hall at Mi Na. 'Welcome,' he said. There was nobody else in the temple. Mi Na bowed his head slightly and walked slowly towards the monk who had since averted his gaze and closed his eyes. 'Stop,' he said. Mi Na stopped. 'Sit,' he said. Mi Na sat. He mimicked the posture of the monk and closed his eyes. The hall filled with monks the gamut of shapes and sizes and they chanted together and they meditated together.

At the end of the service Mi Na approached the large monk who had been sitting at the front of the hall facing rows and rows of monks and a single line of nuns dressed in white. 'Thank you,' said Mi Na. 'At sunrise,' the large monk began, 'we collect alms from the village.' Mi Na could not conceal his excitement but this had been anticipated by his advisor. 'Not you. Not yet.' Mi Na bore the look of a lost soul. 'You will go to the dining area. It is close to your hut. Instead of turning left as you leave, turn right. At the end of the path you will come to a clearing. The nuns will be preparing the kitchen and the tables for breakfast. They will show you what you need to do. When you have completed your chores you will join us for breakfast. It is important that you know you can spend your time here at the monastery as you please. After the gong sounds in the morning, there is only morning prayer and meditation, the alms walk, breakfast, lunch and afternoon prayer and meditation.' Mi Na nodded his head and thanked the large monk. 'Oh, and one more thing,' he went on. 'You must report at once to your neighbour's hut. He will shave your head. It is too hot to carry around all of that hair and besides you cannot keep it clean here.' Mi Na nodded his head and returned to his quarters to wash his face and have his head shaved.

Feeling decidedly fresher post-shave, Mi Na strode down the rainforest path and out into the dining area. Four stone tables stood in a row under a bamboo shelter. A wooden table was set up to one side, unsheltered by bamboo. The nuns waved Mi Na over to them with smiles as wide as the sun. 'Good morning,' said Mi Na. The nuns laughed as one. 'No good morning for you!' Afraid of confusion striking as it had become accustomed to at the most inopportune moments of his journey, Mi Na simply stood and smiled. But for once no one was confused. 'You see the leaves?' asked the most elderly of the nuns. He could see the leaves. They were everywhere, covering the paths of the dining area, the tables and the stools. 'Sweep the leaves into the flowerbeds. Well, what are you waiting for! Here is the broom! Sweep!'

Mi Na took the broom in his hands and swept without blinking. His arms and legs pushed and pulled against the motion of the brush's bristles as though they were automated. In no time, the dining area was free of leaves. The nuns were impressed and the most elderly of them presented Mi Na with a small banana. 'For night time. You are not allowed to eat then but you are new here. You will need it tonight.' Mi Na offered his hands to her and she put the banana in them. 'Now take it back to your hut! Quickly! Before the monks return from alms walk!' Mi Na did as he was told and returned to the dining area for breakfast. He sat in front of a large bowl of noodle soup with no chicken or pork or beef and savoured the scent of the coriander and chilli. A smaller bowl containing sticky rice was laid down next to him by the large monk. 'You did well today. Tomorrow you will walk with us. But first you must obtain the correct garments from your neighbour's hut. Please make sure you do this by nightfall.' Mi Na nodded. He chewed his noodles and slurped his soup and made sure he completed his sole remaining task of the day.

Many months went by and Mi Na arose to the sound of the gong several hours before sunrise. He attended morning prayer and meditation, collected alms from the village, ate breakfast and lunch with the other monks and attended afternoon prayer and meditation. After some time he stopped attending lunch for his stomach was still full with breakfast. He came and went as he pleased until one day the large monk took him to one side after morning prayer and meditation. 'How is meditation going for you, Mi Na?' It was going well aside from the pain so Mi Na told the large monk of the pain. 'Ah, yes, the pain. Now, when you experience the pain you will instinctively try to resist it. This is normal. But this does not have to be normal!' he laughed. 'So next time you feel the pain, dwell on the pain and the pain will cease.' Mi Na did as he was told and the large monk was right, the pain ceased, and it ceased sooner and sooner each and every time. Many more months went by and Mi Na decided it was time to go home. This time, however, he did not feel the urge to leave, nor did he wait to be washed by a wave of euphoria. Mi Na thought of nothing and every last sinew of his body was still. He returned home and swept the floor of his restaurant with his soul for all of eternity.

Truth Teachers

Students convened to discuss the work of a master storyteller. 'This novel was his attempt at an epic,' said a bookish girl. Thick-rimmed spectacles slid down a shiny nose. A well-dressed boy agreed – 'It is his Odyssey.' Nasu rolled his eyes. 'What kind of person wears a scarf indoors?' he wondered. The professor reminded them that they were not alone by clearing his throat in a telegraphed manner – 'Ahem.' He scanned the room.

'Nasu, what do you think?'

'About what, exactly?'

'About the author's place in literary history, of course.'

The student sighed. 'I don't care about that. I want to know why the children have gourds where their heads are supposed to be. One is a pumpkinhead and the other has a longer, greener head!'

The class held its breath. The bookish girl adjusted a beret and the boy loosened his scarf. The professor looked stern.

'The man was mad,' he said.

Before someone could respond, the bell rang and class was

dismissed. There was talk of exams but Nasu had already ducked out. On his way home, a little old lady needed directions.

'Excuse me, where is the library?'

'Straight ahead, you can't miss it.'

The lady walked on without so much as a smile.

'What do you hope to find there?'

She turned to face Nasu, though she did not look him in the eye. 'The truth, dear.'

That night, Nasu did not sleep. He sat cross-legged on a tatami mat that spanned the length of his room. A candle flame illuminated a small book collection, which fitted neatly into an improvised bookcase. 'The truth?' he said. 'If only they could handle it! I see only fear. Fear of authority. Fear of making mistakes. Fear of oneself.' The words Literary Theory caught the light. The flame danced with vigour. 'The best books did not spring from painstaking study but from living. Doing. Acting.' The young man was in a state of fervour. He stood up on the mat. 'This city is only of interest to timid students and zombielike tourists. I must go to a place in the sun and learn to act. I will commit to the moment and bend that moment to my will. No longer can I waste time intellectualising. To hell with perpetual analysis!' He found his holdall, its leather stiff from inactivity, and packed it with pastel shirts, yellow, blue and green. Among them, he tossed a stone engraved with a pictogram of a monk sitting cross-legged. 'Mindfulness is important,' he thought. 'But it must be applied, lest it fall foul of analysis like everything else.' He zipped up the bag and flung it over a shoulder. Outside, a neighbourhood adjusted to morning and shadows passed along the pavement. In a puff of smoke, his father appeared.

'They are asleep,' he said. 'Where are you going with that bag?'

'A place in the sun – I want to learn to act.'

At this, his father smiled kindly and knowingly. 'Those people are crazy but at least they are alive.'

A long flight over land and sea and Nasu was again met by morning. This one had a different complexion. Blue skies proliferated. A vast sandy beach stretched into the distance. He took off his shoes and socks and rolled up his trousers. An elderly couple played checkers, shaded from the sun by parasols. A young boy pursued pocket money playing violin with a flourish when a bill touched down in his hat. All manner of wheels weaved along the walkway beneath boots, boards and bikes. Even a unicycle could be seen. Nasu was wonderstruck by a myriad of movements. He skipped along the beach brushed by an ocean breeze and soothed by the sight of surfers riding waves. His skin was bronzed and his hair turned golden. Soon he arrived at a hostel by the pier. A little old lady greeted him.

'I'm Kym, spelled with a Y, not an I.' She stood no taller than his chest dressed in a black leotard, her back straight as an arrow. She retrieved a pencil from behind an ear with a nimble flick of the wrist and started to write. 'What brings you 'round these parts?'

'I want to learn to act.'

Kym stopped writing. 'You're not ready for acting! First you've got to get out of your head and into your body.' She danced around her subject and assessed it. 'He is strong. Likely quite quick too,' she said. 'Do you train in a gym?'

Nasu shook his head.

'Good, lots of bad habits are picked up in those places. I see you have a weakness in your left ankle.'

'Yes, I do!'

Kym sat down. 'Breakfast begins at seven and ends at eleven, you can make it today if you move along now. Here is your key. We're in low season so you can stay as long as you like. There's someone in that room at the moment.'

'Thank you, Kym. Tell me – how did you know my ankle is weak?'

'You are imbalanced,' she said. 'If you'd like to take this conversation further, join my movement masterclass on the rooftop tonight. It's signposted The Method Theatre.'

Nasu spent the day at the beach and pondered the class. 'Maybe it is some sort of meditation,' he thought. 'The woman is an ageless marvel, I'm sure she can teach me something.' The sun sank below the horizon and painted the sky pink. Observers became silhouettes. It was his cue to get ready. Back at the hostel, his roommate introduced herself. 'I'm Angelina. Nice to meet you, Nasu. Kym mentioned you.' Stars twinkled over the makeshift theatre, which was exposed to the elements, like the scent of an indiscernible foodstuff fried in fat. The steady thud of a heavy bassline vibrated through the walls of a neighbouring building. Kym stood legs apart and hands on hips. 'Class in session. Sit.' Nasu noticed a steel chair and sat down on it. Angelina did likewise. 'Close your eyes. Let your arms hang by your sides. Let your head drop forward on to your chest.' The teacher guided them from head to toe and they alleviated tension systematically. When she reached her wrist, Angelina let out a shrill exhalation. She was instructed to commit to the release with greater conviction and she howled. 'Good, Angelina.' Nasu was encouraged to do the same when he approached his ankle and he obliged with a thunderous yell. 'Very good, Nasu.' Class continued in this vein until they were relaxed. 'Open your eyes. Stand.' The teacher twirled a long bamboo stick. 'Hold it between yourselves.' Angelina tossed the stick at Nasu, who caught it on a pointer finger and moved it into an upright orientation. Then he lofted the stick and she took it back with a little finger. 'Enough of that! Hold it between you. Angelina, recite some lines. Nasu, respond, improvise.' Through the night, they balanced sticks, juggled balls and supported one another. Eventually, class drifted toward a natural end.

'Thank you for your commitment tonight,' said Kym, pulling a woollen jumper over her shoulders.

'A question, please,' said Nasu. 'How does this relate to acting?'

'The work is layered,' she explained. 'You rehearse lines till they are totally natural and you practice movements till they are second nature too.'

'Sure, but what about the emotional and psychological side?'

'We don't do that here. Besides, you've work to do before you can go there!'

Several weeks passed and Nasu attended class at the Method Theatre. Sometimes Angelina was present and other times she was not. One morning, Nasu smoked with a surfer. He noticed Angelina hanging from the rooftop. 'Someone is dangling her by a wrist!' he cried. His face drained of colour. The surfer placed a hand on his shoulder. 'Chill out, dude. Can't you see her smiling?' Angelina grinned from ear to ear. 'It's a trust exercise or something, I guess. Anyway, dude, chill.' Nasu went to his room and packed his bag. He left the hostel and made for the main road. 'I move more freely now but I've learned all I can here, these people are too relaxed,' he mused. A taxi stopped and the driver rolled down a window. A symmetrical face revealed itself. A short straight nose was decorated by a tiny stud.

'Get in the front – dogs in the back,' she said.

Nasu got in the car. He was struck by the smaller dog's eye, which bled. 'What happened to —'

'Pika. Boo attacked her. She's half blind.'

The day pulsated with unrelenting heat. The thermostat touched a hundred. The driver adjusted the air-conditioning unit on the dashboard.

'Where are we headed?' she asked.

'Downtown. I need a change of scenery.'

A cluster of skyscrapers seemed lost in the desert landscape. There were vehicles as far as the eye could see. She fiddled with the stereo. Music faded out. Then a man and a woman debated and a reporter made claims about the truth. The driver suggested they stop at a drive-thru for a burger. Nasu was not hungry but he agreed anyway.

'In-N-Out. Animal style,' she said.

'What is animal style?'

Pika barked and Boo did too. Night would descend before the taxi arrived downtown.

Nasu set foot on a stained sidewalk outside a record store. A stocky man approached. He had sharp cheekbones resembling a pair of pickaxes.

'I've got AIDS,' he screamed.

The driver got out of the car and slammed the door – 'Hey, loser, get a job!'

Nasu was stunned. 'I can't help,' he said. 'I'm not a doctor.'

The man laughed from the depths of his diaphragm.

'Are you kidding me right now? Druj!' The driver had recognised an old friend.

'Yeah, girl. I don't have AIDS, only playing.'

Nasu watched on as they caught up. He contemplated how one could make a false claim so emphatically – 'The emotion is true and the commitment to it is unequivocal.' The driver departed the scene.

'How did you do that?' asked Nasu. 'I totally believed it.'

'That's because I felt it,' said Druj. 'As an actor, I consider my body to be my instrument. Everything we've experienced is lurking within, locked away. That's how we deal with life.'

'I don't want to keep my feelings bottled up, I'm ready to use them.'

Druj nodded a single time. He smiled with all of his being. Then his face became as serious as seriousness itself. 'Come to my class at the Magic Theatre. It's in the basement under the record store. Tuesday and Thursday from eleven.'

'At night?'

Druj nodded a single time. 'I've got to go now.'

Nasu stood on the stained sidewalk until there was a chill in the air. He checked in at a hostel and slept soundly, despite the din downtown. 'Things will be great,' he dreamed. 'Downtown.'

Nasu spent the next day smoking cigarettes and playing pool. The sun beat down and bleached his whiskers. Many a conversation came and went but he struggled to engage with anyone or anything. He could only pot ball after ball. The clock struck eleven and he made his way through the record store to the Magic Theatre. Druj sat centre stage on a back-to-front steel chair. His baseball cap was in the traditional orientation to shield his eyes from the spotlight. 'I'd like to begin tonight's class with a very warm welcome to our newest recruit.' Nasu joined a ragtag pair of actors on stage. A young man with floppy hair and a ghostlike complexion displayed a tattoo of an owl on his chest. An extraordinarily tall woman with long blonde hair completed the line-up. Druj sized up the trio and scratched a pectoral. 'It's playtime,' he said. He stowed his chair behind a velvet curtain and returned with a boombox. 'This is the music of my people. I want to shake off the day and get into my body. Who cares what it looks like? Let's dance!' He flicked a switch and voices could be heard. Some laughed. Others screeched in agony. A frenzied fusion of instruments chimed in and the teacher let each one seep into his body, as though through his very skin. He jigged and jived in a way so fluid yet jerky, so beautiful yet grotesque, that it was impossible to look away. The disparate amateurs followed exhibiting varying degrees of authenticity. Nasu was hot and sweaty by the end and Druj thanked him for his commitment. 'This is a safe space. I'm glad to see Nasu is already comfortable here in the Magic Theatre.' The theatre was truly magical. Druj led his charges through an array of exercises intended to dislodge one's innermost feelings. At one stage, the teacher played a monkey, which he did with unswerving conviction and an uncanny attention to detail. Just when it seemed he had completely and utterly inhabited the mind and body of a primate, he reassumed a human stance. 'Now you go!' All manner of beasts took to the stage: a llama, a lion and a leprechaun. 'Let's stick to animals,' called Druj, orchestrating the class according to his every whim. 'Love the fear, Miss Llama! You're scared of Mr Lion, aren't you? Let's hear that roar!' Nasu roared from the depths of his diaphragm and did so with such conviction that he even surprised himself. The other animals dashed behind the curtain and hid. 'Great work. Let's call it. Shake it off. One thing before you head – I run a slam poetry event every Sunday. If you want to be part of it, get writing. Make it the truth or forget about it.' The group gradually came to and disbanded into the night. Outside, Nasu and the man with an owl tattoo smoked.

'What's slam poetry?'

'It's spoken word. Not necessarily rhyming and stuff, more how we really speak, you know? Oh, by the way, I'm Kevin. It's Nasu, right?' The men bumped fists and went separate ways.

Nasu, Kevin and Druj continued to meet at the Magic Theatre. Sometimes the extraordinarily tall woman with long blonde hair was there and other times she was not. She was working on a poem and wanted to perform on Sunday should her schedule free up. 'That's fine,' Druj would say. 'Just make it the truth.' Nasu revelled in the classes, which became ever more intimate. One time, the actors brought in precious possessions to hone their concentration skills. 'Sometimes there's a rowdy crowd in a theatre,' said Druj. 'Film sets are invariably chaotic places. We need to concentrate so that we can summon the required emotion at will.' He emptied a drawstring sack of special objects on to the stage. There was a framed photograph of his niece. A leather-bound book. A necklace of beads. Nasu took a stone from his pocket. It was engraved with a pictogram of a monk. He held the stone in the palm of his hand and learned to evoke long lost emotions by retracing steps to the past. After some practice, he was able to summon amusement and anger. Then all the emotions flowed. In time, he did not need the stone at all.

The Magic Theatre was at capacity on Sunday night. It burst at the seams with actors of stage and screen, poets and writers, musical artists and even a dancer or two. The theatre hummed with anticipation. Druj and his clan stood arm in arm behind the curtain. 'It's showtime. I want you to go out there and tell the truth, however it looks.' Tell the truth they did. The truth about rape. The truth about drug addiction. The truth about war. The poems were well written and honest. The performances were punctuated by moments of authentic emotion. There was a standing ovation at the end. But Nasu was unsatisfied. He confided in Kevin after the show.

'As thrilling as it was, that's not my idea of truth.'

Kevin lit Nasu's cigarette and then his own. 'How do you mean?'

'I dream of playing a character because characters are archetypes, free from the awkward nitty gritty of real life. They instantiate the truth more purely than any of us.'

Kevin appeared to understand the rub. 'So, like, what you're saying is, characters are more truthful because they're totally unfiltered?'

Nasu nodded. 'We were honest tonight but not truthful. How could we be? We represented ourselves. The whole charade smacked of ego.' The men put out their cigarettes and Kevin suggested they go for a drive. Nasu retrieved his bag from the hostel.

'You're welcome to stay at my place for as long as you need,' said Kevin.

'Thanks. I'm more interested in a drink right now, though.' They drove into the night leaving the Magic Theatre behind.

A desolate landscape ached with nothingness. Traffic lights flipped from red to green. Kevin burned along deserted roads, block after block, lapping up the monotony.

'So, you wanna be an actor?' he said.

'I want to learn to act,' said Nasu.

A neon sign flashed LIQUOR. They took a timeout and picked up a large green bottle and shared it on the roadside, accompanied by towering palm trees, slender trunks swaying, leaves tossed, lost in the darkness. By now in a neighbourhood with unstained sidewalks, they happened on a saxophone solo that trickled out of a bar named Hardware and into the street to greet them. They ordered liquor, neat, and watched a man of mountainous proportions dance with his instrument. He became one with its brass. The music was so sweet that it defied all wisdom. An old dame nursed a glass of water at the next table. 'Commitment to the moment,' she whispered. Tears emerged in her eyes, luminous as the moon. She let a single tear drop into her glass. She wiped away a second before it could fall. 'That's Asha, she was in a hit show about the mob, remember?' Nasu did not. 'Anyway, this place is cool but it's not really my vibe. So I'm gonna, like, head.' Kevin departed the scene. Asha turned to the next table.

'You see that, kid? Truth is truth is truth.'

Nasu nodded a single time.

'Whatever you do in this town of vice and virtue – well, mainly vice – don't fall into the trap. What use is trust if it's abused? Who cares about honesty if it's a mere indulgence of the ego?'

Nasu nodded a single time.

'Look, kid, I see you licking that poison off your lips. I was you once. But our work is about control.'

He put the glass down.

'You are relaxed in the body and concentrated in the mind,' she continued. 'The question is – are you ready to commit to the moment?'

Nasu squinted through the dim lounge. 'I'm ready to commit to the moment and bend that moment to my will.'

Asha frowned. 'Light touch, kid, light touch.' She smiled kindly and knowingly. 'If you're as serious as you seem, you'll join me at Marilyn's. It's a theatre next door. I've got to get some sleep, you should too. See you tomorrow.' Nasu stumbled out of the bar. He would pass out at some time or other.

'The stuff's poison,' growled Asha. She was occupied in the control room at the summit of the theatre, demonstrating lighting protocol to a young actress. 'This one's the main spotlight,' she said. 'You don't need to move it. Just turn it on and dim it using the dial if you like.'

'OK, got it.'

Nasu was blinded and jumped to his feet. Golden letters glimmered. They spelled MARILYN'S. The actress joined him on stage. She had a glassy stare like a discarded marionette no longer of interest to its master.

'Kat is working on a character called Madeline,' said the teacher. 'She's unwell. Never leaves the house. It's haunted. Et cetera.'

'You are Roderick,' said Kat. She handed over a script annotated with words like fear, terror and beat change. 'My last two partners quit, they couldn't hack it. You will be fine. Don't overthink it.'

Nasu scanned the pages. He learned that Roderick takes a trip to visit Madeline and the character unravels over the course of the play. Nasu and Kat began to hang out. They would meet at nightfall and walk around residential neighbourhoods, smoking cigarettes. Kat observed that Nasu did not smoke them to the end.

'Why don't you finish cigarettes?' she asked.

'I don't like to,' he said.

One time they were outside a burger joint and Nasu asked if she was hungry.

'I don't eat meat,' she said.

'Why not?'

Kat stared at her shoes. 'I don't like to.'

They bonded in this way and rarely rehearsed lines. They reported to Asha and showed her their work whenever they made progress. The teacher would reiterate truth is truth is truth. She guided them toward the method. Then, one magical day, they met at Marilyn's. Roderick entered stage left. Madeline waited centre stage. She stared into the spotlight, her eyes glazed over, her body stiff. They danced a dark tango. It was a twisted tale. Minds were lost. Ghosts engulfed them. They emerged on the other side. 'Madeline!' called Roderick. 'Madeline!' he called again. 'Madeline!' Her eyes twitched. He dropped to his knees. Asha appeared in a puff of smoke. 'Keep sacred the art of acting. You're about to embark on a beautiful journey.' The roof of Marilyn's theatre opened and Nasu ascended. He flew home over land and sea.

Mad Man

The final leaf of autumn had fallen and Sami was free to leave the asylum. Conditions of release were as follows: rest and medicate. Work was discouraged. The stipulations applied for a minimum of three years. According to a psychiatrist, a healthy and productive life would be impossible without medication. 'It was summer,' thought Sami. 'It was hot.' He dropped the pills into a bin. Making his way down the street, he reflected on the advice – 'There's no rest for the wicked!' He stopped outside the job centre and rolled a cigarette. Truth be told, Sami was far from a wicked individual. To the dismay of medical professionals, his mood could not be predicted, nor his behaviour brought under control, whatever the cocktail of drugs they administered. The man was not a textbook case. Following weeks of observation and analysis, doctors concluded that he was not a threat to himself or others. He was neither suicidal nor a menace to society. 'If only someone had read one of my stories,' he said with a sigh, crunching the cigarette end underfoot among fallen leaves.

A peculiar scent hovered over the waiting room, sterile yet

human. Fans hummed and keyboards clicked. A young woman tended to three children. An old man slept in the corner. Sami took a seat and clutched his ticket, number one hundred and eighty. Number one hundred and seventy-seven was called. The young woman was uninterested and the old man snored. Staff flanked the room, though no meetings were taking place. A telephone rang and the call was transferred to another department. Sami took a drink from a water cooler and read a sign on the wall – 'Please wait for a job seeking professional to call you.' He had always wondered what happens in these places. Number one hundred and eighty was called.

'Good morning. I'm Margaret, your job seeking professional. How can I be of assistance?'

He declared himself available to begin working at once. The job did not matter. 'I'm open-minded,' he said.

Margaret yawned. 'Let me bring up your file.' She turned to a computer screen and took a sip of tea. 'I can see this is your first time at the job centre. I can also see you have received medical advice to refrain from work.'

Sami outlined his travails and Margaret was sympathetic.

'That is all well and good,' she said. 'But we only offer advice here, not jobs.'

'What else does it say on my file?'

She clicked and scrolled. 'It says you may be entitled to financial benefits due to your medical condition.'

Sami groaned.

'Christmas is coming, dear. We all need a little rest from time to time.'

Spurred into action, he rushed home. His wardrobe was barren. In summer, he had worn out lots of clothes and given away most of the rest. All that remained was a charcoal-grey suit and a white shirt with grass stains. A pair of plimsolls caught his attention. 'Not sure how these got here, flimsy but unused.' He got dressed in a flash. Then he packed a holdall with socks and underwear. There was still plenty of room so he filled it out with items that could prove useful on the journey ahead: a notebook, a pencil, a box of matches and his passport.

Sitting at the station, Sami awaited a train that would take him to the continent. 'Blacklisted,' he mused. A grin grew over his gaunt face and adrenaline coursed. 'If I am of no use here, I will travel east till I find my calling.' His mind wandered to grand boulevards, statues of unknown heroes, the horrors of war and humankind's capacity to rebuild. Our protagonist was not short on confidence. Especially if we consider that he spent his final penny on a train ticket. It was the attitude that had landed him in the asylum. He dwelled on the events that resulted in his loss of freedom that summer. 'I was too open before – too trusting. More guarded this time – more pragmatic. Mistakes are fine, just don't make the same ones twice.' There was no doubting his spirit, which had survived the ordeal intact. Sami was not a proud person but he believed in himself. To be clear, he did not believe he was capable of doing anything, or even very much at all. Rather, he believed his spirit to be good and strong. Moreover, it was his and his alone. It was responsible for anything of value he experienced. To subdue it was not an option. If society could not accept this, he would try another society. It was with this conviction that he boarded a train to the continent.

Sometime between late afternoon and early evening, the cloudy period neglected by a city slinking into winter, he awoke to the scent of baked goods. 'I was going to wake you,' came the voice of an elegantly dressed stranger in the next seat. 'But I did not need to,' she said with a shrug. Before he could thank her, the lady had closed her coat, navy-blue, and darted along the aisle, vanishing into the night. Stumbling into the light, Sami was dazzled. Café heaters, cinema signs, candlelit bedrooms and even humble street lamps acknowledged one another and mingled until they grew bored and turned their attention elsewhere, lending clarity or providing privacy in cahoots with the night. Sami had a special relationship with this city. He never visited for long and this is perhaps why the streets felt fresh every time. He did not care to analyse the magic for fear it would dissolve. He trusted this city as young children trust their mothers. He felt safe in the moment and relinquished any desire to control it. Strolling at a brisk pace, he recalled summer and its sunlight that renders our light unnecessary. 'You do not have a coat?' came a voice from a café. Turning to the terrace, Sami was met by cigarette smoke and a blast of heat. 'Maybe in the bag?' He shook his head. A lady in a navy-blue coat smiled. 'Only underwear in there?' He nodded. 'Take a seat. It is cold tonight.' He hesitated. 'Oh, do you have somewhere to be?' The café buzzed with chatter. Its patrons intoxicated themselves a sip at a time from miniature cups and glasses. A waiter with impeccable posture appeared when required and at no other time. The lady in the navy-blue coat became acquainted with Sami and they smoked together.

'Good evening. Something for you, madame?'

She took a small glass of white wine and insisted he join her. 'I spent all my money on the ticket,' he said and she giggled.

'I do not believe you!' The terrace bathed in neon orange light, its heat lifting jackets and unbuttoning shirts as though from the sun itself. 'Why did you come here?' she asked.

'Often, when I don't know what to do, I come here. The last time was in summer. I experienced an artistic breakthrough at home but there was no one to share it with. So, I came here.'

The lady pouted. 'What did you do?'

Sami told her the story. He had alighted a train to the scent of baked goods. Then he strolled at a leisurely pace. The sun was high in the sky and one could tell the time according to its position. The city rocked with abandon. Locals and visitors celebrated summer as one, basking in its glory. On a bridge, a street performer had intrigued him. A black and white clad mime was performing a routine of expressions and gestures stitched together by subtle movements invisible to the untrained eye. Sami proceeded to mimic the mime with unerring accuracy and a crowd gathered.

'Ugh! I hate mimes,' cried the lady.

'Most people do, but they are highly skilled.'

'Are you a mime?' she asked.

'No! I am not.'

Two glasses of wine appeared. 'Please continue.'

It was all happening – families enjoyed picnics, friends played ball and lovers danced. Sami carved a path through the city of moments. He painted with painters and sang with singers. A fountain of energy, he seldom slept and subsisted on little.

'Were you on drugs?' asked the lady.

'I was not.'

Nevertheless, the effect of the artistic breakthrough was considerable. Our protagonist had managed to write a story with fluency, each sentence imbued with truth, after years without success. Such was the sense of satisfaction, he had been overwhelmed by a cascade of emotions. The waterfall, unblocked by relief, crashed over rivers of joy and euphoria and drained into the ocean of love itself.

'So you are a writer?'

He shrugged.

'You were running wild,' she said. 'It was hot.' They gazed out at the street and savoured a pause, punctured by a clap of thunder. Rain flowed over awnings. 'Why did you come here?' she asked. 'You must have an aim.'

'I'm looking for work.'

The café came to a standstill. Heaters were off. 'I have a job for you.'

By now it is clear that our protagonist was not destined to find respectable work in this city. It is, for better or worse, the city of moments. Fortunately, he had low expectations. He also had not a cent to his name and his plimsolls were about to be soaked. Having excused himself, he made for the toilet. He washed his hands and face. Then he admired three framed water-colour paintings hanging in a row. Two were images of the city of moments but the third seemed to be an image of another city. He did not recognise it but he could tell that this city had suffered. He returned to the terrace, where the lady waited under a large umbrella. 'You can stay at my place tonight but I need to stop by the office first.' The pair walked arm in arm. Engulfed in a downpour, they went left and right and left. Red and green spilled from traffic lights and streaked across cobblestones. Headlights scattered. He marched to the beat of her drum. He rolled a cigarette but he could not smoke it. He could only feel his feet, cold and wet. His legs were starting to fail him. 'We'll be there soon,' she said. The office was on the top floor of an old building. A narrow stairwell housed a rickety lift, which only travelled up halfway. They would need to climb a spiral staircase of steep stone steps to make it to the very top. Sami was fading. He summoned his last ounce of strength to open a window on the landing. He breathed in the cold night air. He took off his plimsolls and socks and wrung them out into the street below. Then he laid out his things, one by one, on top of a radiator. He left the window ajar. On seeing his feet, cut and bruised, the lady shed a tear. 'Oh no,' she whispered. In the office, she removed the navy-blue coat to reveal a white uniform. He stared at her but she did nothing. He collapsed in a heap on the floor. A warm blanket was draped over him and he snuggled into it. Kids lose a ball to the river and he dives in to retrieve it. The sun dries him. A waiter gives him a sandwich and recommends an arch under which he can sleep. Sirens prevent him from sleeping. There is no sun at night. There is no heat. There is only the moon in the sky. It is beautiful but one cannot tell the time according to its position.

A woman introduced herself – 'No pressure, Sami. I am here to help you.' She asked him questions about appetite and sleep. He said that he ate adequately and slept sufficiently. She wanted to know what he had been up to and he told her about his writing and the fun he was having. A pair of nurses entered. They asked the same questions and he gave the same answers. A doctor performed a similar ritual. Then he carried out a host of tests to determine whether substance abuse was responsible for the patient's behaviour. A nurse was delighted when the results came back negative. 'This will go well for you,' she said. The doctor noted that the patient's potassium levels were low.

'Would you be open to receiving medication for the problem?'

'Can't I just have a banana?'

'Of course you can.' He marked a notepad with a quick flick of the wrist.

The nurses returned. 'How are you feeling, Sami?' said one.

'You seem a little irritable,' said the other.

'I just need a cigarette.'

'Of course, you've been in here a while. One more question and you can go for a smoke. Is that all right?'

He nodded.

'Would you be open to psychiatric care?'

He shook his head.

One nurse gulped and the other marked a notepad.

'How about that cigarette?'

Sami was escorted out of the office by the lady in the navy-blue coat. She watched him put on his socks and shoes. They walked down the stairs arm in arm. Then she pressed a button to call the lift.

'How are you feeling?' she said.

'Great. How about you?'

She hesitated. The lift arrived and she stepped inside. The doors closed. 'Oh no!'

Two at a time, Sami skipped down the steep stone steps. He revelled in the rhythm of his hips giving way. He relished the tired vibrations of the rickety lift and the lady trapped within. Outside, he looked left and right and chose right. Sirens sounded. He sauntered and rolled a cigarette and then he lit it. The front door to the old building swung open. He jogged and smoked and slid over cobbles. A baker asked for fire and received a matchbox and a single matchstick. 'Thank you. Good day!' Sirens grew louder. Turning left, he lengthened his strides. He glided along the street barely touching the ground. He flicked the cigarette into a puddle. A tourist asked for directions to the tower. 'Follow the river – that way.' Sirens whined and pedestrians winced. Turning right, he shortened his strides. The café was opening.

'Good day. Something for you, sir?'

'A coffee and the toilet, please.'

'OK. The toilet is right ahead.' Sirens reached fever pitch.

Sometime later, police arrived at the café. Two men were accompanied by a nurse and the lady in the navy-blue coat. An officer questioned the waiter and another searched the premises. The waiter was not much help.

'Every day people come here. They take coffee. Some smoke,' he said with a shrug.

'Was anybody behaving unusually this morning?'

The waiter raised his eyebrows. 'Unusually?' he said. 'What would be unusual to you, Mr Officer?'

Meanwhile, an officer had made his way to the toilet. He washed his hands and face. Then he admired two framed water-colour paintings hanging in a row. They were images of the city of moments. To the side, there was a nail. The area around the nail was less faded than the rest of the wall. He dried his hands and exited.

Not every city is so pleasantly lit as the one we have just visited. But light can deceive. The next destination on our itinerary may lack the charm of the city of moments but it has a mystique all of its own. Cafés exist here too, as do cinemas. However, locales cannot be delineated by a gradient of heat or colour, only cool shades of grey permeate. The city echoes with howling winds and chatter is muffled. This narrator is unsure if intoxication occurs on its avenues. In fact, it is unclear whether anyone is harboured within its walls at all. Well, it is not my role to reconcile these facts! I am certain our protagonist will do his utmost to navigate a significant city – the city of divisions.

Sami was in good spirits. Not one to bear a grudge, he shrugged off recent events. 'They are just doing their jobs,' he thought. 'I need one of those.' First he had to familiarise himself with a new culture. A café appeared open. Large glasses with handles stood empty. Ash trays held cigarette butts. An old television set played a football match and its flickering black and white image captivated him for a short while. He stepped behind the bar and took his fill of water from a tap. Then he performed his ablutions and left. Strolling down a broad boulevard lined by trees, their branches bare, he wondered where everyone could be. 'Probably at work.' He walked up to a newspaper stand and glanced at the headlines. The words were longer than those in his own language but bore some resemblance. They made reference to the Olympic Games, though the edition in focus was one long since passed. He crept up to the kiosk and peeked through the window. 'No one home.' Sami wandered in search of locals without success. Eventually, he came to the end of the boulevard where he would find a library. Its reception was unguarded. It was not unusual for our protagonist to frequent libraries. He was a curious individual. Although he appreciated the company of others, he was equally happy to commune with people from the past. Walls of books put him at ease. He noticed an anthology by his favourite author and recognised a couple of titles – The City, The Poet – though he could not understand the stories. Restoring the book to the shelf, he was moved by the mountain of knowledge he had yet to obtain and the universe beyond, which would forever remain unknown. He remembered childhood and a treasured atlas. The countries of the world had fascinated him. First he studied their flags. Then he discovered capital cities. How impressive that some were so large! How silly that others were so small! He indulged in these memories and smiled at how distant they felt. 'Everywhere is essentially the same,' he thought. 'Still, I need to learn about this place.' So he selected a hefty book titled A History of the City of Divisions, and a dictionary from the language section, and off to work he went.

The story was familiar. An agreement was made. It was broken. Violence and destruction ensued. People suffered. The less they had, the more they lost. But everybody lost. Then it was time to rebuild. However, there is a twist in the tale of this particular city. While other cities were able to rebuild as one, this one would do so as two. A wall was erected and a city within a city came to be. Divided, the city rebuilt and marched towards an uncertain future, its past preserved and its trauma crystallised. Sami translated the book one word at a time until he could resist sleep no longer. He rested his head on its pages. The scent of worn paper soothed him. His childhood atlas is well used. Next to it are children's encyclopaedias. One is about dinosaurs. Another is about the solar system. A storybook tells of a boy who travels from one planet to the next. Sami sits cross-legged on his bed. He hugs a teddy bear. They met on the day he was born. The teddy is threadbare. There is noise beyond the wall. Someone is struggling. Footsteps approach.

Sami woke up with a hand on his shoulder. A man in a black uniform escorted him out of the library and into a vehicle. They cruised through the city. Sami peered out of a window and glimpsed a pigeon. The wall came into view.

'Where is everyone?' he asked.

The man glared at his mirror.

'Such a lifeless city, why?'

The man's eyes quivered.

'I'm just curious.'

The vehicle stopped. 'Do you know who you're talking to?'

Sami stared blankly.

The man began to sweat. 'I demand respect!' he shouted.

'I don't mean any disrespect, I just have some questions.'

'I ask the questions!'

The man seethed and hail stones crashed against the vehicle. Before long, they arrived at a concrete structure. A guard frisked Sami. Then he was led through a series of doors, which opened inwards. Black uniforms shadowed one another. In a small room at the end of a corridor, a woman in a white uniform was waiting. She sat at a table decorated by a cactus plant. It was established that Sami had committed three transgressions.

'When I arrived, there was no one around. I stepped inside a café hoping to find someone,' he explained. 'I drank from the tap and washed my hands.'

'Did anyone let you?'

He shook his head. Then he told her about the news stand – 'I only glanced at the headlines.'

'Were you given permission?'

Again, he shook his head. Finally, he recounted the story of the library – 'I just wanted to learn.' He protested in vain.

'Was access granted?'

The man took a seat next to the woman. 'We want to help you,' he said. 'But you must follow the rules.'

'What are they?'

The man grew angry. 'First, no questions!' he yelled. 'Second, do not speak unless spoken to. Third, complete and utter silence at all other times.' He shook violently and his eyes bulged from his face.

The woman suggested that it would be best not to touch anything in the building unless absolutely necessary.

'Why not?'

'Remember the first rule,' she whispered.

Sami was shown to a room. A window opened an inch inwards and a single bed had been made up with fresh sheets. He had neighbours on both sides. There was a dining hall with round tables and meals would be served three times a day. The building had an inner courtyard adorned by rose bushes and a patch of turf was in use as a football pitch. 'If only it were possible to play in silence,' he thought. Dinner time came and he met a neighbour. He had not taken any food and sat with his eyes closed. When he opened them he greeted Sami with a nod. 'Mo,' he mouthed. The man was youthful and blessed with a warm smile. Sami consumed a portion of meat and potatoes and then dessert. He took seconds. Mo sat opposite. He had a bottle of milk that he did not drink from. He spent dinner time reading a small green book. The men used expressions and gestures to agree to meet at nightfall.

Lying on his bed, Sami gazed at a starry sky. 'Where am I? Why am I here? What is wrong with questions?' The reverie was interrupted by a knock at the wall. He checked the corridor. The door to his right was ajar. He tiptoed in. Mo was kneeling on a patterned rug. Things were strewn: clothes, tobacco and a football.

'You play?' asked Sami.

Mo shook his head. 'My friend gave it to me. It is good to share.' A generous soul, he provided his neighbour with a supply of tobacco, papers and filters.

'We can't smoke here, can we?'

'No, but you can walk outside if you obey the rules.'

'Really?'

'Yes. It's nice here.'

'Wouldn't it be nicer if we could ask questions?'

'No. It's peaceful this way.'

The men would get to know each other. Sami learned of Mo's faith and took to reading the green book as there were no others in the building. 'My book is banned too,' confessed Mo. One night, he gifted his friend a rainbow-coloured scarf. 'Winter is coming,' he said. The smoking rule soon materialised. For a week of good behaviour, Sami received permission to walk in the community after lunch under the supervision of a guard. He discovered that people existed in the city after all. Each walk revealed a different neighbourhood. One was occupied entirely by men. Another contained only women. There were separate areas for children and the elderly. When Sami returned he would ask Mo about what he had seen. But Mo was no use. He simply said 'praise be.'

'Don't you want to leave this place some day?' Sami would ask.

'I will,' Mo would say. 'When it is decided.'

One evening, Mo was not at dinner. Someone else sat in his place. 'Joe,' he mouthed. Joe played with his food and sized up Sami. Then he invited him to his room. Night fell and Sami awaited a knock at the wall. He lay on his bed and stared at the stars. 'I wish I could leave, but where would I go? What about the wall?' The knock came. He checked the corridor and the coast was clear. He tiptoed into the room to his left. Joe sat on a plastic chair. He wore a raincoat and a cap.

'What's your story?' he asked.

So Sami told him everything. 'I wanted to write but I was blocked. One day, it happened – I could do it! I rode the crest of a wave.'

Joe smiled. 'I bet they thought you were mad.'

Sami shrugged. 'That was in summertime. I've moved on since then. I'm looking for work.' Yes, he told him everything – about the café, the news stand and the library. He told him of the man in black and the woman in white. 'They don't let you speak. How can you understand something if you can't question it?'

Joe stood up and removed his cap. 'You can,' he said. Over the coming weeks, he spoke about the men in black and the women in white. 'They curtail our freedom,' he would say. 'I used to work as a builder. I put up the wall,' he confessed.

'The one that surrounds the city?'

'Yes. I didn't know better. Nowadays, I raise awareness about the group that commissioned it. One legal battle ends and another begins.'

'Don't you miss freedom?' Sami would ask.

'No,' Joe would say. 'But I understand why you do.'

Indeed, he had heard his story before. It was the story of an artist. In time, Sami would summon the courage to ask about the wall and he learned that it obstructs no one. One night, Joe gifted his friend a pair of heavy black boots. 'Next time you go for a smoke, just walk away,' he said. 'Good luck.' The following day, Sami walked to the station and boarded a train to the east.

Taking a seat by the window, he rested his weary legs. They were not used to carrying such heavy boots. He took off the rainbow scarf and held it in his lap. A whistle shrieked and steel wheels screeched. The locomotive pulled and the passengers rocked forward. Everyone dressed in white shirts and charcoal-grey suits. Huffing and puffing, the train rolled out of the station. Pistons and valves thumped. The engine wheezed and they breezed along the tracks. It was in this way that our protagonist continued across the continent in search of work. He watched fields fly by. Steam streaked clouds. Sleet fell. How he wished he could see something. Alas, even fields faded from view. Wagons rumbled. The temperature rose. Soot clogged the air. The smell of sausages wafted round the carriage. Heads rattled against window panes. Bombs fall. Cities razed to the ground. A man enters. 'Curly hair?' he says. Sami checks his head – shaved. His great-grandfather takes a seat across the aisle. He makes sure no one is looking, then he eats a sausage in three bites. He does not notice Sami. He travels in the opposite direction – west. They hurtle past each other. People push wheelbarrows under blue skies. There is a lot of work to do. A small piece of wall stands. People are indifferent to the piece of wall. It survives.

'Last stop – all passengers alight.' Sami wrapped up in his scarf and advanced through a station. Signs were written in an unfamiliar script. 'I must have been asleep a while,' he thought. Grand chandeliers swayed from marble ceilings. Fur coats jostled for position. Diamonds gleamed. Sami sensed opportunity. However, he had arrived with nothing. With trepidation, he approached a booth signposted Immigration. As he waits in line and ponders his fate, I will tell you about the city in which our protagonist has ended up. It is without hyperbole that I describe the mother of all cities. Her scale cannot be grasped, she lacks a beginning and is missing an end. To call her eternal would barely raise an eyebrow of a local. Unlike others, she does not advertise herself. Her aura beams in every direction rendering neighbouring settlements irrelevant. The phenomenon occurs along a radius so vast that this narrator does not care to measure it. Even when one escapes her sphere of influence, the majestic impression she leaves stays long in the memory. She lives at the junction of space and time.

'Passport,' requested an official. He opened the document and turned to a computer screen. 'We have been expecting you, mister.'

Sami frowned.

'What is the purpose of your visit?'

'Work.'

The official scanned the screen. 'No work for writers here,' he said. 'We have availability in the teaching sector.'

'Teaching what?'

'Your language.'

'I've never done that before.'

'You will be trained.'

And so it was agreed, Sami would join a company that specialises in language teaching. He thanked the official, who stamped his passport and waved him on his way. Outside the station, a man held up a sign marked SAMI. His nose was red with cold. Sami rolled a cigarette and by the time he was through his fingers had frozen. 'Not cold – mild,' said the driver. The men trampled their cigarettes into slush. 'You – home.' Sami did not question the seamless nature of the operation. 'I'm due a break,' he thought. Spectacular sights kept him entertained on the trip. Great golden domes shone like giant baubles. A labyrinth of monastery walls criss-crossed. A red clock tower revealed itself. Squinting to tell the time, Sami could only see snow. It was the first of winter. In the early hours, the car arrived at its destination. Someone was waiting outside an apartment block. His hat was thick with powdery snow. 'Sasha – welcome!' He showed Sami inside. They shook off snow by stamping their feet and brushing their shoulders and it melted on contact with the floor. The new recruit would be stationed in a room behind a heavy-duty door. There was a single bed and a window, which opened outwards. Sasha presented a card. 'For train – always credit.'

Sami slept soundly. The city of his dreams slumbered under a blanket of snow. When morning came he opened the window and stuck his head outside. Floating flakes fell faster and faster and he watched them until he became dizzy. Then he got ready for work. On the way to the station his boots disappeared with every step. An army of men worked to remove snow from walkways, roads and building tops. Still, snow fell. At least the tracks were clear. Trains sped from one underground palace to the next. Each had its own personality. Magical mosaic. Powerful painting. Sophisticated stonework. Passengers absorbed as much heat as they could. 'Next stop – alight for the big theatre.' Sami stepped off the train and an escalator carried him upwards. He exited the station and marched through the city to the central office of his new employer. Above its doors, a sign read LANGCO. Langco was a gargantuan corporation. Its headquarters were housed in a monstrous structure, a maze of skyscrapers interconnected by bridges. Sami spent the day traversing this leviathan. At 10AM, he was expected at the recruitment department. An office of women named Anastasia received him. 'We are so happy to have you at Langco,' said one Anastasia and her co-workers squealed with laughter. A document was presented. 'Please sign here.' Sami did as he was told. At 11AM, he was due at the finance department for a meeting with Olga. 'We are all called Olga,' she said. 'Please sign here and here.' At midday, they broke for lunch. Sami took a coffee from a vending machine. That afternoon, he would complete Teaching 101 led by Tatiana and her team.

'What now?' he asked.

'Now you are certified,' she said. 'You need to meet the boss. He has the contract.'

An enormous desk stood in the office of the company head. From it rose a tower of paper. A pen appeared. 'Before you sign,' came a voice, 'you must decide whether you are ready for the cold.' Sami signed the contract. 'Leave your passport,' came the voice. He did as he was told.

Our protagonist did not take to the job like a duck to water. First he was assigned a class of children. He tried to teach them the days of the week but they ran amok. So he was tasked with teenagers instead. A lesson on the animal kingdom and they never showed up again. Then he taught adults. It was with them that he discovered his vocation. The subject matter of textbooks receded into the background and students took centre stage. The teacher tailored classes to individuals and their goals became his. He cherished the work. Not once did his mind drift to fiction. He had neither the time nor the energy. 'All I want to do is teach,' he would say. 'It is honest work.' His ability and work ethic were such that the hierarchy would maintain a constant supply of students. Soon his schedule was full. Work followed sleep and sleep followed work. Sami did not dream and the cold deepened. He marched through the mother of all cities and gave all of himself to Langco. One class was especially intense. She was a formidable student, a mother of three, who worked full-time as a language teacher. Together, they would hone grammar and refine pronunciation.

'What did you do before you became a teacher?' she asked.

He told her that he had written stories.

'Once a writer, always a writer,' she would say.

He suggested suitable homework. Then he would drink at a pub and the final train carried him home.

One afternoon, Sami sat in a square on his break. He watched birds circle the spires of a cathedral and they soiled the sacred building. It was not the first time. An old lady exclaimed and crossed herself. Nearby, a statue of a poet was untouched. 'The birds respect him,' thought Sami. He made his way to school for the next class but the students did not show up. The teacher arrived on time to every class on his schedule to no avail. At the end of the day, he drank at the pub and caught the final train. A letter waited at home. It summoned him to the central office. Classes had been cancelled and schools were closed until further notice. Pay could no longer be guaranteed. That night Sami dreamed. He is in the city of moments running wild. He is in the city of divisions walking away. He is in the mother of all cities living his dreams. Morning came and he got ready for work. He put on his boots and wrapped up in his scarf. Into the cold, he marched. The train brought him to the big theatre. Then he headed for the central offices of Langco. It was business as usual in administration. Anastasia believed that everything would soon return to normal.

'We must be patient,' she said.

Olga was also optimistic – 'There is no need to worry.'

Tatiana agreed – 'You are a great teacher, stay!'

Sami was not so sure. 'I would like to speak to the boss,' he said.

The head of Langco was busy. Teachers had filed complaints. Some thought they could be made redundant. Others feared they could be evicted from their living quarters. It was even speculated that the city itself could shut down. 'What about the contract?' called one. 'The boss says it's invalid!' cried another. Sami had heard enough. He knocked on the door.

'Come in,' came a voice.

He approached the desk. 'I can't stay without pay.'

'Then you must leave,' came the voice.

'May I have my passport?'

'Yes, you may. But first you must win a duel.' A pistol appeared.

'Isn't that a bit old-fashioned?'

Laughter echoed. Paper fluttered. Our protagonist took the pistol in his hands. He turned and took three paces towards the door. A shadow moved across the wall. A drawer creaked. He spun on his heels and pulled the trigger. Snowy steppes. Crunchy hay. Running wild. Icy lakes. Sauna steam. Swimming free. Grassy hills. Fragrant fir. Flying home.